THE ENDERMEN
INVASION

THE ENDERMEN INVASION

A MINECRAFT GAMER'S ADVENTURE
BOOK THREE

Winter Morgan

Sky Pony Press
New York

Sky Pony Press books may be purchased in bulk at special discounts for sales
promotion, corporate gifts, fund-raising, or educational purposes. Special
editions can also be created to specifications. For details, contact the Special
Sales Department, Sky Pony Press, 307 West 36th Street, 11th Floor,
New York, NY 10018 or info@skyhorsepublishing.com.

Sky Pony® is a registered trademark of Skyhorse Publishing, Inc.®,
a Delaware corporation.

Minecraft® is a registered trademark of Notch Development AB.
The Minecraft game is copyright © Mojang AB.

Visit our website at www.skyponypress.com.

10 9 8 7 6 5 4 3 2

Manufactured in Canada, October 2014
This product conforms to CPSIA 2008

Library of Congress Cataloging-in-Publication Data is available on file.

Cover photo credit Megan Miller

Print ISBN: 978-1-63450-088-3
Ebook ISBN: 978-1-63450-089-0

TABLE OF CONTENTS

1

THE INVITATION

Steve received an invitation to participate in a building competition.

"They said there are only five contestants," Steve told his friend Max. "We have to build a house, and they're going to judge who constructed the best house."

Max was excited for Steve. "Wow! Only five. That's awesome that you were chosen!"

"The contest is in a few days, and it's pretty far away," Steve explained as he handed Max a map from his inventory. "I want you to come with me."

Max smiled. "I'll go. What an adventure! I can't wait to cheer for you when you win."

"I'm not sure I'll win, but I am honored to be a part of this competition," said Steve.

Lucy and Henry walked into Steve's living room, and Max told the group about Steve.

"The building competition taking place on Mushroom Island?" asked Lucy.

Max looked at the map. "Yes."

"I've heard about it! It's very impressive! Congratulations!" exclaimed Lucy.

"What do you build?" asked Henry.

"There are five contestants and each one has to build a house. Then the judges choose the best one," explained Steve.

"Wow, that sounds really exciting," said Henry.

"I want you guys to come with me," said Steve.

Everyone agreed they would join Steve. This would be an adventure, and they wanted to support their friend.

"We need to celebrate tonight," Henry told the group.

Steve realized that his friends' excitement was distracting him. He wanted to win the competition and he knew he had to stay focused, but he didn't want to hurt his friends' feelings. There were so many things Steve needed to do to prepare for the competition. He had ideas for the home he wanted to build and knew it wasn't going to be easy. Yet, Steve wanted to show his friends that he cared about them and was thrilled they were going to join him.

"I have to go to the village and get supplies for the competition. I need to make sure my inventory is full. I don't think we'll have time to celebrate, but once the competition is over I promise to throw the biggest party ever," Steve told them.

"Yes, we have to celebrate your victory!" exclaimed Lucy.

"Lucy," said Steve, "I told you, one of the other four people chosen might be the winner. But I'm just glad to be a part of it—and that you guys are joining me!"

"And you'll need a party if you lose. It will cheer you up," Henry pointed out.

"That's not nice," Max told Henry.

"It's fine. I want to have a party. I think it'll be fun," said Steve.

There was a knock on the door. It was Steve's neighbor Kyra. Before she could even enter the house, Lucy told Kyra the good news. Kyra tried to smile for Steve, but it was a forced smile; you could see a few tears in her eyes.

"Are you okay?" asked Lucy.

"I was hoping I'd get chosen for the competition. I entered, but I wasn't picked," Kyra told them with wet eyes.

Steve comforted Kyra. "Kyra, you are an awesome builder. Why don't you come with us? This year it's my turn, but you might be chosen next year. I think you'll enjoy coming with us."

"Kyra, look at the map," said Max. "There are so many fun places to see on the way to Mushroom Island."

"We'll need a builder like you. You're an expert at building boats, and we'll need them to travel to the island," said Steve.

"When the judges see the boat you've built, I'm sure you'll be picked next time," added Lucy.

Kyra stopped crying. "With friends like you guys, I feel like I've won the best contest in the world. You are awesome. I think I will go with you, Steve. It was wrong of me to just think of myself. I'm so happy for you."

"So you'll build us boats?" asked Steve.

"Yes!" Kyra told him.

"Let's go to see Eliot, the blacksmith, and trade wheat for supplies," said Steve.

Steve and Kyra walked toward the local village and when they got to Eliot's blacksmith shop, Steve opened the door.

"Congratulations, Steve," said Eliot, "I heard you were chosen for the building competition. Everyone in the village is talking about it."

"Thanks!" replied Steve, "And Kyra and my other friends are going to join me. She's going to help build the boats that will get us to Mushroom Island."

"That's an important job," Eliot told Kyra. "You're a good friend, Kyra."

Steve and Kyra traded with Eliot and then made their way back to Steve's house.

"Are you nervous?" Kyra asked as the two walked through the fields toward Steve's wheat farm.

"I've never been to Mushroom Island, and you know that I'm not the best when it comes to traveling. I like to stick close to home. But I'm excited to build a house for the competition. I have lots of great ideas."

"I've never been to Mushroom Island either, but there aren't any hostile mobs there, so it seems like a really safe place," said Kyra.

"I think they chose a place without hostile mobs so the contestants could just focus on building the best house without worrying about getting attacked," said Steve.

"Oh no!" Kyra called out. "Look!" Kyra pointed to a witch hut in front of them.

"I wonder what the judges would think of her hut," Steve joked as they walked past her hut and hoped she wouldn't emerge.

"*Shhh!*" Kyra hissed at Steve as they made their way toward the wheat farm. "I don't think she heard us."

But they weren't safe! Within seconds, a witch ran from the hut toward Steve and Kyra. The witch drank a potion as her evil eyes focused on her two victims.

"Run!" Steve yelled at Kyra, but they weren't fast enough. The witch was right behind them. Steve took out his diamond sword and leapt toward the witch, who held up a potion. As they battled, the witch splashed Steve with her potion.

"Oh no!" Kyra called out.

"Ugh!" Steve said weakly. Kyra rushed to Steve and gave him milk to help him get his strength back.

The witch sprang toward Kyra, who struck the witch and defeated her.

"Now you'll have the strength to win the competition," said Kyra as she gave Steve more milk.

"I wish it were that simple," Steve told her. "But we need to get back; it's getting dark and hostile mobs will be on the prowl."

Kyra and Steve sprinted, but they still had a while before they were back at the farm and it was already dusk.

Boom! There was a blast in the distance.

"What was that?" asked Kyra.

"I hope it wasn't my house."

Kyra and Steve rushed toward the wheat farm, hoping everything was okay so they could start their journey to the competition.

2
READING MAPS

There was a patch of burnt grass by Henry's feet.

"What happened?" asked Steve.

"There was a creeper!" Lucy told them. "Luckily Max destroyed it."

"I defeated a skeleton," announced Henry proudly.

"You don't have to brag, Henry," joked Lucy.

Steve lit a torch. "It's getting too dark to be outside," he said. "Let's get to sleep. Tomorrow we have to start the trip to Mushroom Island. We need our energy. Kyra, you can stay here with us if you would like."

"Thanks," said Kyra.

The group entered the living room but as they walked toward their beds, Max pointed to a pair of red eyes on the living room wall.

"It's a spider," warned Kyra. The spider was camouflaged in the dark room, but its eyes stood out. The spider climbed up the wall of the home.

Henry took out his bow and arrow and aimed at the spider that was about to pounce on the group. His arrow struck the spider and destroyed it.

"Good job, Henry!" said Steve.

The gang got into their beds and fell asleep. They dreamed of the adventures they would have the next day.

When they woke up, Lucy roasted a chicken she had hunted, and everyone ate apples.

"We need to have a full food bar before we go on the trip," said Steve, as they feasted on an enormous breakfast.

The competition was very far away, and Max had spent a long time studying the map to make sure they wouldn't get lost. "We also have to fill up our inventory," he said. "This trip isn't going to be easy. And I'm hoping we can find some treasure on the way."

"Max!" exclaimed Lucy, "this isn't a treasure hunting trip. It's about helping Steve get to the competition and cheering him on."

The group followed Max as he led them toward Mushroom Island. As they trekked through what seemed like endless grass fields, Kyra asked, "What are we going to do for shelter at night?"

"I came prepared," replied Steve, "I have extra wood so we can make a shelter each night."

"Wood? That could be burned down in a minute by a creeper. I thought you were cautious, Steve," said Henry.

"It's our only option. We're going to have to risk it," said Steve.

"Wow!" Lucy was shocked. "I like the new Steve. You're finally taking risks."

"I want to get to the competition." Steve was sincere. He was excited to build the home for the contest. He had so many ideas, and he couldn't wait to work on his entry.

Rufus barked as the group walked out the door. "Should we bring him?" asked Kyra, and the dog looked at Steve.

"I think bringing Rufus would be a bit too much for us. He can stay here and play with Snuggles." Steve was heartbroken, he wanted to bring Rufus and Snuggles, but it was a long trip, and he knew they'd be safer at home.

"The map!" Max called out to the group. "I can't find it!"

"Do you think somebody took it?" asked Henry.

Steve was worried; he tried to hold back his tears. "If we don't have the map, we won't make it to the competition on time and I'll be forced to give up my spot . . ."

"I looked at it so long, maybe I can help us find our way there from my memory?" suggested Max.

"I don't think that's the best idea, Max," Lucy said.

Max was annoyed. "Do you have any other ideas?"

"We have to find that map." Steve went back into his house and started to search through his inventory.

"Everyone, check your inventory," Henry instructed the group.

"I know the trip started out going past the fields and the village and toward the jungle," Max told them.

Steve sat down beside Rufus. "We can't do it without a map," he said.

"I'm sorry," said Max. "I feel like this is all my fault. I was the one with the map."

"It's not your fault," Steve told him. "But now we can't go to the contest."

Max urged his friend not to give up. "Yes, we can!" he said.

"I also remember looking at the map, and Max is right—we go through the jungle to the water. Mushroom Island is just off the jungle in the sea," said Henry.

"I'm not going to take a chance getting lost. It's not worth it. We won't make the competition, and who knows if we could ever find our way back home. It's too risky," Steve said sternly.

"Risky? I agreed to go on this trip when you told us that we'd be sleeping in wood houses every night even though we could be killed by a creeper, and now you're giving up just because we lost the map," said Kyra.

"You act like losing the map isn't a big deal! It's the only way we can get to the competition," said Steve.

"After what happened with Thomas and all the griefing he caused us," said Kyra, changing the subject, "I am worried that a griefer stole the map."

"There's nothing we can do about it," said Steve, "and it doesn't matter. I'm not going to the contest."

Lucy had another theory about the missing map. "I bet another contestant stole the map," she said. "They knew you were going to win because they saw your nice house."

"Or Max could have just lost it," added Henry.

"But I have no idea how that would have happened," said Max. He was upset; he didn't want to be responsible for losing the map.

"You can't give up, Steve," Lucy pleaded. "You were so excited about the contest."

Steve sighed, "Let's all check our inventory one more time."

Suddenly Kyra called out, "I have the map!"

Everyone was shocked.

"You didn't hide the map because you weren't chosen and you were jealous, did you?" Henry asked Kyra.

"Henry, how can you ask such a question?" said Lucy. She was upset. "Kyra is our friend."

"No. It just showed up in my inventory," said Kyra. "I wonder how that happened. I hope it wasn't the work of a griefer."

Steve was excited. "It doesn't matter how it got there. Now we can go."

Kyra gave Max the map, and he led them in the direction of the contest. Cows grazed in the meadow, and the trip seemed quite scenic and peaceful until they reached an area where there were so many trees, they couldn't see anything but leaves.

Steve stood a foot from Kyra and called out, "Kyra, where are you?"

"I'm behind the tree," Kyra said. From the sound of her voice, Steve realized she was in front of him and he reached out for her.

"How are we going to make our way out of here?" asked Henry.

"We're lost in the thick of the jungle!" cried Lucy.

"Don't worry, I have the map," Max reassured them.

"Can you read it?" asked Steve.

There was no response.

3

WELCOME TO THE JUNGLE

"**M**ax!" Steve called out.

"I can't see anybody," said Lucy in a quivering voice. "Steve, is everyone here?"

"Everyone, say your name," instructed Steve.

Kyra, Lucy, and Henry called out their names in unison. Max was the only one missing.

"Where's Max?" asked Lucy.

Steve walked slowly through the dense jungle and called out Max's name. He was about to give up when he heard somebody say, "I'm over here." The voice was very faint and Steve wasn't sure it was Max's voice.

"Max is that you?" Steve was hopeful.

"Yes! I found a temple!" Max said, sounding much closer. "I'm walking toward you. I want to help you guys find it."

Lucy was annoyed. They had to get to Steve's competition, and there wasn't any time for treasure hunting. "Was that on the map?" she asked.

"No, it was covered by trees," said Max, "I just stumbled upon it. A jungle temple is very rare. We *have* to go inside and see if there is a treasure chest."

Henry was excited. "We could get emeralds or an enchantment book."

"Do we have time to go into the temple?" Kyra asked the group.

"Yes, we can't pass this up," Steve told them.

"But where is it?" Lucy asked.

Trees surrounded the gang. The trees were enormous; the deep green leaves looked as if they were touching the clouds.

Henry looked up at the trees. "I bet if we climbed up one of these trees, we'd be able to play in the clouds."

"That sounds dangerous," remarked Steve. "Imagine falling from the top of one of those trees."

"Who cares about climbing the tree? I want to find treasure!" Max told them, as he reached Steve.

"I can finally see you!" Steve stood in front of Max.

"I can't see you, Max," said Lucy.

Max took out shears from his inventory and started to cut the leaves, making a path for the group. They followed Max toward the temple.

The jungle temple was made of mossy cobblestone and the gang marveled as they entered the three-story building.

"Watch out for traps," Henry warned them.

They kept their eyes out for any traps or hostile mobs that could be lurking in the temple.

"Treasure is usually on the bottom floor," Lucy pointed out. She led the group.

"Watch out!" Kyra screamed as Lucy almost stepped on a trap door.

"Thanks, Kyra!" said Lucy.

The group walked slowly, watching each step down the stairs to the treasure.

"You can't just take the treasure," Max told the group. "You have to solve the puzzle first."

The room that held the treasure chest had three levers that connected to sticky pistons.

"Which lever should we push?" asked Steve.

Click! Clang! Sounds of creaking bones came from the hall.

"Oh no!" Kyra exclaimed. "There are skeletons."

"Does anybody have a torch?" asked Max.

"No, we're going to have to fight them. Nobody is going to stop me from getting this treasure," Henry told them.

Henry took out his bow and arrow, and Max grabbed his diamond sword. A skeleton crept past the door, and Max leapt toward it with his sword out. As Max struck the skeleton, Henry shot an arrow with his bow and they defeated the hostile mob in this manner.

The group gathered by the treasure chest. "Are there any clues on how to solve this puzzle?" asked Kyra as she stared at the levers.

Steve was afraid of choosing a lever to pull. What if he chose the wrong lever and it set off a TNT explosion? They'd all be destroyed. Steve was annoyed that they found the temple; he wanted to be farther along on their trip to the contest. Treasure hunting wasn't a part of the plan. He had a contest to prepare for. But right now he stood in front of three levers, and if he pulled the correct one, he would be rewarded with countless treasures. But, if chose the wrong one, he'd be destroyed.

Kyra accidentally stepped on the tripwire in the middle of the room and two arrows shot through the air. The gang narrowly avoided being hit by the arrows.

"Is everyone okay?" Steve asked once the arrows stopped flying at them.

"I'm sorry," apologized Kyra.

"It's okay. It's hard to avoid the tripwire. We're treasure hunters, so we've been through this a bunch of times," Henry told her.

"Which lever should we pull?" asked Steve.

Henry took out his pickaxe. "We don't need to pull any levers." With a wallop Henry banged his pickaxe against the wall. "We can break down the wall and get to the treasure chest."

"Or we can just pull this lever." Lucy confidently pulled the middle lever; the chest emerged from the hole in the ground.

Kyra was impressed. "How did you do that?"

"Instinct," said Lucy. She carefully opened the chest to reveal a box filled with gold, emeralds, enchanted books, and . . .

"Yuck!" Max said. There was rotten flesh in the chest.

"At least there are treasures in the chest. Let's just avoid the rotten flesh," said Henry.

The group divided their fortune.

"We can use these emeralds to trade with Eliot the blacksmith when we get back home," remarked Steve.

"These enchanted books will come in handy when we need to enchant a sword," said Kyra.

"*Shhh!*" Lucy hissed. "Do you hear something?"

There were voices coming from above. Somebody else was in the temple, and the gang had to make their escape before they were forced to battle them for their treasure.

"How can we get out of here?" asked Kyra.

"We can make a hole in the wall and get out through there," suggested Max. He took out his pickaxe and started to break down the wall. The others began to join him. They heard footsteps growing closer.

They tried to get to the other side of the wall, but it was too late. A man in a black helmet stood at the door; he pointed a bow and arrow at them.

"I'm the master treasure hunter. Hand over the treasure," shouted the helmeted man.

"Never!" Henry screamed and grabbed his gold sword.

Steve took out his diamond sword and tried to reason with the man. "Don't try to fight us. There are five of us—you'll never win."

"Who said I was alone?" replied the man in the helmet.

4

ALMOST THERE

They didn't know if this stranger in the black helmet was bluffing, and they weren't going to wait around to find out. Steve charged at the man with his diamond sword and stopped him from shooting any of his friends with a bow and arrow.

Four men armed with swords and wearing black helmets emerged from the hall.

"Get them!" Lucy screamed at her friends.

Steve tried to strike the helmeted man, but he sprinted away. Steve caught up to him and held the sword near the man's chest.

"We don't want to fight," Steve told him. "Let us leave with the treasure."

"Never!" the man replied. One of the man's friends lunged at Steve with a gold sword.

Max used his bow and arrow to stop the man with the gold sword.

Clang! The room was filled with the sounds of a sword battle. Henry fought another helmeted man with a gold sword. Lucy took out her bow and arrow and shot an arrow at the man Henry was battling. It struck the man and destroyed him.

"Whoa!" exclaimed Henry. "That was close! I could have been killed by your arrow Lucy."

"But you weren't," Lucy replied as she rushed to help Max and Kyra battle the other sinister hunters.

It was a challenging battle. His enemy was smart and fast, easily missing Steve's strikes. The fight was using a lot of Steve's energy bar, and he needed help.

"I'm so strong I can fight you without a weapon," the evil man in the helmet declared to Steve. "And I'm going to get that treasure. You'll never get out of here alive."

"Yes we will!" Steve took a deep breath, and with all his might he hit the treasure hunter with his beloved diamond sword and defeated the man.

"Help us!" Henry called as he and Max battled another treasure hunter. But the treasure hunter was distracted by his leader's demise and Henry was able to destroy the robber.

There were two men left now. One took out a bow and arrow.

"I have a plan!" Lucy told the group. "Sprint to the hole in the wall!"

The gang dashed toward the wall as the two men followed closely behind. When Lucy saw her friends were making their way to the other side of the wall, she quickly ran to the levers and pulled one and ran as fast as she could.

Boom! TNT exploded and the entire room was destroyed.

"Lucy," Max called out through the smoke. "Are you okay? Did you make it?"

"Yes, I'm here," she replied.

The group made their way through the ashes and climbed up to the first floor of the temple.

"We need to get out of here!" Max told the group as they tried to find an exit.

"I hear more voices," said Kyra.

"This place is overrun with treasure hunters," exclaimed Henry.

Hurrying through the first floor, Steve spotted another treasure hunter with a green helmet.

The treasure hunter took out a bow and arrow.

"Stop!" Steve shouted, "There's no treasure here and no reason to fight us. The treasure was blown up by TNT. And we have nothing for you to steal."

"You're an awful treasure hunter. Anybody would know how to solve the puzzle and get the treasure," the green helmeted treasure hunter remarked as he grabbed his sword and lunged toward Steve.

"Okay, we're bad," replied Steve as he shielded himself from the impact of the sword and struck the treasure hunter, destroying him.

The gang found the exit and headed toward it.

Kyra was shocked. "Wow, Steve, you lied!"

Henry was impressed. "And dude, you destroyed him!"

"I didn't want to fight him," explained Steve.

"I know, but that isn't like you at all," said Kyra.

"Sometimes you have to fight to defend yourself and tell a white lie in order to get out of a bad situation," said Steve, defensively.

"Well, now I don't know if I should trust you, my friend," Henry joked.

The group couldn't tease Steve about his white lie anymore; a green-eyed wild ocelot was charging toward them and distracted them.

"Does anybody have fish?" asked Steve.

Lucy grabbed some fish from her inventory, offering it to the wild spotted ocelot. It ate the fish, and its fur turned black with white paws.

"Aw," Lucy said as the ocelot ate the fish, "it's tame now. I finally have a pet."

"Treasure hunters can't have pets," Henry reminded her. "We live a life on the road."

"Should we take it with us and bring it home to Snuggles?" suggested Steve.

The group didn't know what to do with the tame ocelot.

"I'm going to name it," Lucy said as the ocelot purred. "I'm naming it Jasmine."

Steve knew Lucy had grown fond of that cat. And he also knew that if they didn't get to the water soon, they'd miss the contest. "Lucy, let's take it with us. And I'll keep it on the farm."

As the group walked toward the water with their new pet, Max looked at the map. "I think the quickest way to get to the water is by burning down a section of the jungle. It will take us forever to make it through these trees, but if we burn down some trees, we'll have a flat patch to walk on."

The group agreed, so Steve crafted flint and steel to make fire. They watched the green trees turn red as fire spread through the jungle until there was a path toward the water.

Steve looked out at the vibrant blue water. He couldn't see an island in the distance; it looked as if it went on forever.

"Are you sure this is the right way, Max?" asked Steve. He was nervous they'd get on a boat and be stuck at sea.

"Yes," said Max reassuringly, "we just need some boats."

Kyra began to craft boats for each of her friends.

"I want a pirate ship," requested Max.

"I want a cruise ship," Lucy called out.

"We don't have time for Kyra to make anything that fancy," Steve reminded the group.

"Don't worry guys, I have a bunch of great ideas. You'll get the boats you want."

Kyra worked hard on the boats while Lucy hunted for chickens and cooked for the group before they set off on their journey at sea.

Kyra came over to get a piece of chicken. "I want Max to see his boat," she said.

It was a small wooden pirate ship.

Max tried to talk like a pirate. "Ahoy, matey!" he said. "Thanks, Kyra! I love it!"

Kyra made a small cruise ship for Lucy and matching sailboats for Henry and Steve. She had a small rowboat for herself.

Kyra was excited. "I used command blocks so the boats can move. Let's take a voyage on the high seas!"

"Next stop, Mushroom Island!" announced Lucy. She said goodbye to Jasmine, knowing that the ocelot would teleport once she got to Mushroom Island and that they would be reunited.

Steve looked out at the water from his sailboat. "It's so beautiful here," he said.

Boom! A loud noise instantly disrupted their tranquil voyage.

"Did you hear that?" asked Henry.

"It's thunder!" Steve shouted. He grasped the mast tightly as water flooded the floor of his boat.

"Hold on!" yelled Kyra.

But that was easier said than done when sailing on stormy seas.

5

GETTING TO MUSHROOM ISLAND

Rain and seawater flooded the boats.

"We're going to sink!" Lucy called out in terror.

"Don't worry, we're going to be okay if we just hold on." Kyra knew her boats were well constructed and could withstand a fierce storm.

Lightning flashed across the sky. Steve was scared. "I don't want to be struck."

"Nobody does!" Kyra replied. "Just hold tight. It will pass. I can see the sun."

Steve and the gang didn't believe Kyra. And Steve wasn't sure Kyra even believed herself. But they held on as their boats were battered by the storm and their bodies were showered with rain.

Steve was cold and wet. He wished he were already on Mushroom Island and building his dream house for the contest. As Steve was almost thrown off his boat, he distracted himself with thoughts of the home he would build. It would be extremely waterproof and would be a place where you'd love to take shelter in a storm. His home would be a place everybody would love. He'd make large windows to show off the stunning ocean views from Mushroom Island. Of course, first he had to get there. And as another lightning bolt lit up the night sky, he wondered if he'd ever make it.

"Oh no! The lightning stuck my command block," said Lucy. "My boat isn't working."

"Jump aboard my boat," said Henry as he navigated his sailboat toward Lucy's little cruise ship.

Lucy almost fell into the water as she carefully hopped onto Henry's boat, but Henry held out his hand to steady her. "Thanks, Henry," she said.

Finally the rain stopped, the water became calm, and there wasn't any thunder or lightning to distract them.

"I told you I saw sun," said Kyra.

"I feel bad that the cruise ship was damaged," Lucy said to Kyra.

"It's only a boat. You're my friend. You're a lot more important. I can always craft another boat, but I can't make another you," replied Kyra

The sun was strong as the group sailed toward Mushroom Island.

Steve was both excited and nervous. "I can't believe we're almost there!"

"Do you have an idea of what you're going to build?" asked Max.

"Yes, I hope the judges like it," said Steve anxiously.

"They will," said Henry reassuringly.

"I think that storm took away a lot of my energy," said Steve. "I need to eat before we get to Mushroom Island or I won't be able to make a good house."

"We should fish!" said Kyra. "When it rains, it creates a lot of fish. Let's do it now."

"I've never fished before," confessed Steve. "I have no idea how to do it. I never crafted a fishing rod."

Kyra loved being at sea and had fished many times. "I'll help you," she said.

With Kyra's help, the group crafted rods and waited for the fish to bite. Within seconds, Steve had a fish on his rod.

"Get it quick!" said Kyra. "If not, it will jump off."

"I got one too!" Lucy shouted and reeled the fish in.

"I got salmon!" Max told them. "Yummy!"

"I just reeled in a clownfish!" Henry boasted.

"I didn't get a fish," said Kyra.

"That's too bad," said Henry.

"Don't feel bad for me." Kyra revealed what she had caught on her fishing rod. It was treasure.

"You found treasure!" Lucy beamed.

Kyra showed them. "Yes, an enchanted book."

"Lucky!" said Lucy.

"Look!" said Steve. "I can make out the tip of Mushroom Island."

Keeping their boats very close together, the group sailed slowly toward the island. They stood at the edge of their boats and looked out at the island in the distance.

"I can see other boats docked there," remarked Kyra.

Steve knew those boats were for the other contestants. He was nervous to meet them, but there was no turning back. Their boats were on course to arrive at the island in a short while. Soon he'd be docking next to a group of people who were also expert builders.

The seas remained calm but Steve wasn't. He surveyed the island. They were getting closer, and his stomach felt like there were butterflies flying around in it. This was his first contest. He'd never been invited to participate in anything before. Steve took a deep breath and felt the sun on his face; he told himself that he'd do the best job he could and wouldn't be distracted by the judges or the other contestants.

"We're almost there!" Lucy called out. The shore was visible.

Max pointed at something in the distance. "Look at those large red mushrooms! You can see them from all the way over here."

"Wow. They're so cool!" said Steve. He used to be scared of new things and seldom left his wheat farm, but now he was looking at mushrooms that were taller than him growing on the lush landscape of the island.

They were just a few feet from the dock. Kyra's boat was the first in their line of ships. "Let me dock and I'll help you guys," said Kyra.

Kyra hopped onto the dock. "The boats will be fine here."

"What nice boats. They're certainly unique," a woman dressed in purple told Kyra.

"Thanks!" replied Kyra.

"Are you a contestant in the building competition?" asked the woman in purple.

"No, I'm here for my friend Steve. Are you in the competition?" asked Kyra.

"My name is Lexie. I'm a judge."

Steve, Max, Lucy, and Henry walked onto the dock.

"Steve, this is Lexie. She's one of the judges for the contest."

Steve was nervous. He didn't want to do anything wrong; he wanted the judges to like him. "Nice to meet you, Lexie."

"I can't wait to see what you build, Steve," said Lexie. "And Kyra, these boats are so fantastic. I might hire you to build one for my trip home."

They were on land, the storm was over, and it seemed as if everything was going to be okay.

Vroom! Steve turned around to see a fast boat approaching the dock. *Bang!* It crashed into Steve's rowboat.

"You hit my boat!" Steve called out.

A guy dressed in blue got out of the boat. "My name is Joshua. I'm just here to help my friend Caleb. Sorry about your boat." Although he apologized, Steve felt like Joshua didn't actually care about what he had done.

"Steve, don't worry about the boat," said Kyra. "I'll build you another one."

"Are you a part of the competition?" asked Joshua.

"No, I'm here to help my friend," replied Kyra.

"So you're just like me," said Joshua.

Steve didn't think Joshua was like Kyra at all.

6

JUDGES AND CONTESTANTS

The gang walked onto Mushroom Island, marveling at the enormous mushrooms as they made their way up a steep hill toward a flat patch of land.

"The mushrooms look like giant umbrellas," said Lucy.

"I heard you can build a hut out of them," stated Henry.

"We should do that while you're at the contest," added Lucy.

"It's going to be fun building here, right Steve?" asked Max.

"Yes, I'm glad that I'm finally on an island without creepers, zombies, and all of those hostile mobs that make building anything a serious challenge," said Steve.

What Steve didn't tell his friends was that despite the absence of hostile mobs, he was still scared. He had never had anyone judge his work before, and he was afraid he'd lose the competition. Steve couldn't believe that he had spent so much time looking forward to his contest and soon it would be over and he might go home without winning. The idea of the contest was a lot more fun than actually being there. This was going to be hard work and he was nervous. Steve wanted to do a good job.

The group walked farther onto Mushroom Island and looked at the empty landscape in front of them.

"I wonder where the competition is being held," remarked Kyra.

In the distance a man and woman, both dressed in purple, walked toward them.

"I bet they know," said Steve.

The man and woman in purple introduced themselves. "I'm Jonathan. This is Sylvia. You must be Steve. We're the judges. We'd like to invite you to a party. You can meet the other contestants."

"Can I bring my friends?" asked Steve.

"Of course," said Sylvia, "the more the merrier."

Jonathan and Sylvia led the group to their accommodations. It was a huge building with lots of beds.

"These are the dorms. You will stay here with the other contestants and their friends," said Sylvia, showing them their beds.

Steve could see Joshua talking to his friend. He assumed it was Caleb. Steve walked over to them.

"Hi, Joshua," said Steve.

"Caleb, I told you about Steve. I accidentally hit his boat," said Joshua. "I'm so sorry, Steve. I feel really bad about destroying your boat."

Joshua sounded sincere, and Steve wondered if he'd originally misjudged this speed demon.

"We will give you the tools to craft a new boat," Caleb assured Steve.

"That's very nice of you guys," he replied.

A voice boomed through the room. It was the judges, all dressed in purple, speaking in unison: "*The party will begin shortly. Everyone meet on the stage outside the dorms.*"

The group exited the dorms and made their way toward the stage. The contestants were asked up on stage.

"These are five very talented contestants chosen from hundreds of entries," said Sylvia. Her voice was loud enough for everyone to hear.

The guests watched as Sylvia introduced each competitor.

"Contestants. When I say your name, please approach the front of the stage." She announced the first contestant, "Caleb."

Caleb walked to the front of the stage.

Sylvia introduced Georgia. Steve looked over at her. Georgia was dressed in yellow. Steve realized he was next. He had never stood in front of an audience before. He was nervous.

"Steve."

He turned red and quickly went to stand behind Georgia.

Sylvia introduced the last two contestants, Eli and Sarah. Finally, the contestants were allowed to leave the stage. Steve hated having the spotlight on him.

"Wow, Steve. I didn't realize there were so many people who entered the contest. How great that you were picked," Lucy told him.

Steve didn't want to make a fuss because he knew Kyra also wanted to be a part of the contest.

Steve looked down and then over to Kyra. "Guess so," he said.

"Contestants, please walk to the left of the stage," instructed Lexie.

Steve joined the other contestants. Eli and Georgia walked over to introduce themselves.

"Hi, I'm Eli."

"I'm Georgia. I just want to wish you good luck."

"Yes, good luck." Steve could hardly talk, he was so anxious about the competition, which was to begin shortly.

"Are you nervous?" asked Georgia kindly.

"Can you tell? Yes, I am," admitted Steve.

"So am I," Georgia told him as Sarah walked toward them.

"Me too," added Eli. He put his head down as he spoke. He seemed embarrassed to admit that he was nervous.

"Are you guys talking about how nervous you are?" asked Sarah.

Steve laughed. "Yes."

"So are we," said Sarah as she pointed to Caleb. "I think we should all just try and do our best."

Steve loved seeing how other people built homes. "Although we are competing against each other,

I'm also excited to see what types of houses you guys create," he said.

"Let's all promise each other to try our hardest and have fun," said Georgia.

They promised.

Caleb walked over with Joshua.

"I thought this area was only for the contestants," Sarah said to Caleb. He put his head down and walked away. Steve thought he heard Caleb mutter something, but he wasn't sure.

The judges blew a whistle, and everybody turned around. Jonathan announced the rules of the contest. "Each contestant has one week to build a house. If you don't have enough supplies, feel free to mine on Mushroom Island. But remember, your home must be completely done at the end of one week."

Sylvia added, "We will judge the contest on originality and durability."

Lexie said, "We all know Mushroom Island doesn't have the hostile mobs that roam and devastate most of the biomes in the Overworld, but we want this home to survive anywhere. Show us your best work!"

"Good luck contestants!" Jonathan told the group.

"And let the games begin!" Sylvia announced.

The contest had begun. Steve went to the patch of land where he would spend the next week building the home. Maybe there wasn't a hostile mob, but he had a new enemy now. Time. Every minute he wasn't building the home was a minute lost in this weeklong battle of the builders. Only one person would come out the first place winner.

7

MINES AND MOOSHROOMS

Steve checked his supplies. He checked again. He looked through his inventory a third time. He couldn't believe it. His coal was missing. Steve thought he had brought everything. He needed the coal to make bricks for his cobblestone home.

"How could I forget coal?" Steve asked himself. He was annoyed.

Steve had no other choice. He had to mine. He would lose building time, but if he didn't mine, there would be no house. He had spotted a mineshaft; he put his helmet on, grabbed his pickaxe, and went mining.

Steve used a torch to light the dark tunnel. He was excited to mine without having to worry about cave spiders or skeletons attacking him. He dug through the dirt surface looking for a layer deep within the ground that housed coal.

"Steve," a voice called out.

Steve looked up from the deep crater. "Yes?"

"It's Georgia." She held a pickaxe.

"Did you forget something, too?" Steve asked as he continued to mine; he didn't have any time to waste for conversations.

"Yes, coal." Georgia began to mine as well.

"So did I," said Steve.

"Really? That's odd." Georgia found some coal. "Good, at least there is a lot of coal down here."

Steve showed Georgia the coal he found in the mine. "I know," he said.

"I was sure I had coal in my inventory. I'm the type of person who always comes prepared. Maybe I was just nervous and that's why I forgot it," said Georgia.

"Me, too! I was also sure I had coal. I checked everything twice," said Steve as he gathered the last of the coal he needed for his bricks.

"Do you think somebody stole our coal?" asked Georgia.

"Do you think they are trying to ruin our chances of winning?" asked Steve. He was worried Georgia could be right. He had already been a victim to the griefer Thomas, and he knew what type of damage bad people could do.

"Yes," Georgia replied as she mined.

"I have all of my coal. I have to go," said Steve, "But if you see anything that seems peculiar, let me know and we can alert the judges."

"Maybe we should tell the judges about the coal?"

"No," replied Steve. "You never know if they'll take points off for us forgetting supplies. Maybe nobody stole our coal. Maybe we just forgot it." Steve walked toward the exit carrying coal, and saw Sarah entering.

"Did you also forget coal?" Sarah asked Steve.

"Yes, and you'll find Georgia looking for coal, too," Steve told her.

"It's funny that we all forgot coal. Pre-contest jitters, I guess," said Sarah.

"I think it's too much of a coincidence that we all forgot our coal. I'm beginning to suspect that somebody is up to no good," said Steve.

"Who would do something like that?" asked Sarah.

"Somebody who wants us to lose," replied Steve.

"That would be awful," said Sarah as she walked farther into the mine.

"Go get your coal. You don't have any time to waste," said Steve. "And I'll keep my eye out for any other suspicious acts."

"Thanks," Sarah said as she began to mine.

Now that Steve had his coal, there was nothing stopping him from building his dream home. He walked to his allotted spot and began to work on the foundation for the home. He was excited to start on the project. After working without a break for quite a while, Steve began to feel tired. He needed to increase his energy, so he went in search of food.

Steve was a wheat farmer and hated hunting animals. He had grown to love all the sheep and pigs on his farm, and it always bothered him when he had to kill a chicken. Lucy was the hunter of the bunch. She was always cooking chicken and steak.

Steve walked around the island in search of food, but he couldn't find anything worth eating. As he walked back to the land where he was building his home, he spotted mooshrooms bathing in the water beside the house. Steve was very thirsty and hungry; he wanted to milk the mooshroom for its mushroom stew. Steve walked over to the mooshroom and placed a bowl by the passive animal. He also took out his shears and sheared another mooshroom, turning it into a cow. He saved the mushrooms from the mooshroom-turned-cow and milked the cow with a bucket. Steve now had an endless supply of mushroom stew and milk. He was thrilled.

With the coal he had mined, he was able to create all the bricks he needed. Steve was making good progress with the house and felt as if nothing could stop him. Even if there was a griefer stealing coal, he could still succeed and build his home. Steve finished the foundation for his home and began to craft a small wall of bricks. He was happy with the way the house looked.

Dusk was approaching as Steve worked on the first wall of the home. Since there were no hostile mobs and nobody would attack him, Steve would be able to sacrifice a part of his sleep and work into the dark night. He placed a torch on the wall of the home.

Steve heard a deep growl in the distance. He could have sworn it was an Enderman. However, he told himself he was hearing things, because there were no hostile mobs in the mushroom biome.

The raspy sounds grew louder. Steve turned around to find two Endermen behind him. He tried not staring or provoking them, but it was too late. They were teleporting toward Steve.

8
THE INVASION

The two Endermen stood with their mouths open. Their calls grew louder. Steve sprinted through the pitch-black night sky, trying to remember his way toward the water. He could hear the sounds of the Endermen as they teleported. He wasn't fast enough! He ran faster, but they were right behind him. He hoped he was close to the water. The Endermen made a piercing sound as they landed in front of Steve. The only thing left for him to do was jump. He jumped off the cliff and into the deep blue water.

Splash! The water felt refreshing as Steve swam along the coast with nothing but the moon to light his way through the sea.

Steve could still hear the menacing sounds from the Endermen waiting to attack Steve. They teleported toward him.

Plop! The two Endermen landed in the water and were destroyed.

Steve could hear cries coming from the distance, and he quickly swam to the shore to investigate.

"Help!" the voice called out.

Steve hurried toward the voice. As he got closer he realized it was Georgia.

The contestants weren't allowed to enter another contestant's area where they were constructing their homes. It was in the rules. If a contestant entered another's space, they were immediately disqualified. The judges didn't want any of the contestants stealing each other's ideas. But Steve knew Georgia was in trouble and he had to break the rules to save her.

He could see three Endermen teleporting toward Georgia. He grabbed a bow and arrow from his inventory and shot at the Endermen, striking one of them. It didn't even bother the Enderman. Endermen were hard to destroy, since they had a lot of energy.

The Endermen saw Steve with his bow and arrow and left Georgia to teleport toward Steve. Steve took out his diamond sword but knew he was helpless. There was no way he could battle three Endermen.

Although it was a losing battle, he had to fight. Steve lunged at an Enderman with his sword. Just when he thought he was about to be killed, Georgia rushed over with buckets of water, pouring them on the Endermen and destroying them.

"Thanks! You saved me." Steve was relieved but also wary. He kept an eye open for Endermen in the area.

"No, you saved me," replied Georgia.

"I think we saved each other," Steve said and then quickly picked up the Ender Peals that were dropped when the Endermen were destroyed.

"What are you doing?" inquired Georgia.

"Take some of these; they're very helpful if you need to teleport away from a hostile mob." Steve handed the Ender Pearls to Georgia. "Just don't eat them—they are very toxic and can lower your health bar."

"What other hostile mobs will I need to teleport from here? I thought the Mushroom Islands didn't have hostile mobs," said Georgia. "So why were there Endermen here?"

Steve was also confused by the appearance of the Endermen. "I have no idea, Georgia, but I'm guessing it's the same reason we all seemed to be missing our coal. It must be the work of a griefer."

"Do you think it's another contestant?"

"I don't know," answered Steve, "but I'm going to find out. This griefer isn't going to disrupt the competition. And the contest will be a fair one. No tricks."

"I agree with you. And I'll do anything to help you find the griefer," Georgia said as the night began to fade.

"I have to leave now. I don't want to accidentally see any part of your house," explained Steve, and he headed toward his house.

As Steve worked on his home, a siren boomed through the island. After the siren stopped, Sylvia made an announcement: "All contestants please report to the stage."

As Steve walked to the stage, he wondered what the meeting was about. However, when reached the stage, he knew what Sylvia was going to say. He quickly noted there were only four contestants, including him. One was missing!

Sylvia stood on the stage with her fellow judges, Lexie and Jonathan. Sylvia spoke. "Last night we had a very rare Endermen attack. We lost one of our players—Eli. He is now back in his home and won't be able to compete because, it's too far for him to travel back to the island."

Steve was shocked and upset. If he hadn't jumped in the water, he could have died and respawned at his home, too.

"That's awful," said Sarah. "Last night I also saw two Endermen, but luckily I had a pumpkin in my inventory and was able to craft a mask and they didn't see me. How did the Endermen get to this island?"

"We have no idea," replied Sylvia forlornly. "Did everyone see Endermen last night?"

Everyone said they did. At once all the contestants started blurting out their Endermen stories. Georgia told the group about Steve's heroic efforts.

"The judges and I have decided that we should all craft pumpkin masks to have on hand so we are ready for another attack," Sylvia told the group. "We're going to get to the bottom of this. If one of you is responsible for summoning Endermen, you will be disqualified from the contest."

"What about Eli? Will anybody take his place?" asked Caleb.

"No," answered Sylvia. "Now the contest is down to four. If we lose any other contestants, the contest will be canceled."

"Canceled?!" Caleb was upset.

"Yes, it's only fair," Sylvia told them.

"Was Eli the only person who was respawned in his home?" asked Steve. He had been so busy building his home; he was worried about his friends Henry, Lucy, Max, and Kyra. What if the Endermen had attacked them?

"What makes us extremely suspicious is that the Endermen only attacked the contestants." Sylvia's voice sent a chill down Steve's spine.

Steve wondered who would want to ruin the contest.

After the meeting, Steve walked back to his home. When he got there, he spotted a small creature with a red eye on the ground by the entrance to his home. It was an Endermite! The invasion wasn't over!

The sun was about to rise and soon the Endermen wouldn't be able to terrorize the players. But Steve knew if there were Endermites, there were still Endermen. It was just a matter of time before they struck again.

Steve destroyed the Endermite with his diamond sword. They were easier to battle than Endermen, but they never traveled alone. Steve grabbed the pumpkin from his inventory but he didn't even have time to craft the mask before the familiar piercing sound of an Enderman teleporting began ringing in his ear. He was in trouble!

9
ENDERMITES

The Enderman landed in front of Steve. Normally Endermen were very passive unless provoked, but these Endermen seemed to be aggressive. Steve wondered if it was the lack of other hostile mobs that made these creepy beasts with purple eyes more potent.

As the Enderman teleported toward Steve, the Endermite crawled by his feet. He had to destroy the Endermite before he battled the Enderman. Luckily Steve's neighbor, Adam, was a potion expert and had given him a bunch of useful potions to take with him on his trip. Steve ran to his chest where he stored the potions and grabbed the Splash Potion of Harming. Steve splashed the potion on the Endermite. The Endermite was destroyed, leaving a trail of purple dust.

Steve spotted another Endermite through the purple haze, and he lunged at the evil bug with his sword. When he looked up, the hostile Enderman stood in front of him. Steve struck it with his sword. The Enderman grew weaker. He hit it again. The Enderman was destroyed. As Steve picked up the Ender Pearl, he saw an army of Endermen heading toward him. Steve ran toward the water, but there were too many Endermen on his trail and his energy bar was low. He wasn't going to make it!

Running toward the shore, Steve comforted himself with thoughts of Snuggles and Rufus. Once he was respawned, he would be back on the wheat farm with his pets and in the comfort of his own bed. He was just about ready to surrender when he heard the cries of an Enderman being destroyed. Steve turned around to see Max, Henry, Lucy, and Kyra dressed in armor and battling the Endermen.

Kyra plunged her gold sword into an Enderman as Lucy struck another.

"Lead them to the water!" Steve shouted to the group as he took out his diamond sword and joined them in battle.

Clash! The sword battle intensified as the group led the Endermen toward the cliff and hoped they'd fall into the water.

They reached the edge!

"Jump!" Steve shouted to the group.

Lucy, Max, Henry, and Kyra jumped into the water. The Endermen followed.

"We're saved!" Lucy called out gleefully.

"You're still in the contest!" Henry told Steve. "This is awesome!"

"I know this must be awful for you, but I had fun fighting the Endermen," said Max. "I was getting kind of bored just sitting around waiting for the contest to be over."

"That's an awful thing to say, Max," said Lucy.

"I have to agree with Max. I liked battling the Endermen with you guys," admitted Henry.

"Well, I'm glad it's over," Steve said, but as they reached the shore, the group realized it wasn't over. It had just begun.

The shoreline was crawling with countless black Endermites emitting a purple aura.

"Don't get out of the water!" Henry warned them. "Not until we have a plan."

Kyra stared at the Endermites. "How are we going to destroy these Endermites? There are hundreds of them!"

"I have a splash potion," Steve told them. "Let's throw it at a bunch and then use our swords."

"This looks like a losing battle, but we can try." Henry's voice quivered as he spoke.

Each armed with a splash potion, the gang walked from the water and threw it at the Endermites, destroying them. Yet the Endermites seemed to respawn instantly.

"How can we win?" Lucy wondered aloud.

In the distance Steve saw Georgia, Caleb, and Sarah heading toward the shore. They were dressed in armor and ready to join the battle.

Georgia, Caleb, and Sarah fought and defeated a bunch of Endermites. As the group destroyed a majority of the evil bugs, they grew more confident of a possible victory, but they still had some doubts.

They were distracted when they heard people call for help. The group wanted to see who was calling to them, but they were too busy battling the Endermites. If they lost concentration, they could lose the battle.

"Help us!" the voices repeatedly cried out.

Within seconds, the judges dashed toward the shoreline, four Endermen following closely behind.

Georgia, Caleb, and Sarah ran toward the Endermen and struck them with their swords. Steve sprinted to Georgia and Sarah, joining them in battle.

Lucy, Max, Henry, and Kyra were defeating the Endermites and soon the shore was emptied of hostile mobs.

Everyone looked at the empty shoreline with relief and exhaustion.

"I need food. My food bar is very low," Steve told the group; he wasn't feeling very well.

"I saw a few mooshrooms over the hill," Georgia told them. "We can milk them for mushroom stew."

The gang walked to the pasture where the mooshrooms were grazing, but they barely had the strength to make it up the hill.

The mooshrooms grazed peacefully. Steve approached one with a bowl and began to milk it. He handed mushroom stew to the group. Once everyone was fed, they began to talk.

"Who would spawn Endermen and Endermites?" asked Sarah.

"Someone who wants to destroy the competition," Sylvia replied.

"But who would want to destroy a competition we worked so hard to get into?" asked Steve.

"There are only four of us left," said Caleb, "and I'll fight any hostile mob in order to keep the contest going."

"Actually, we have some good news," said Lexie. "Eli will be able to make it back here. He will participate in the competition, but he will just build a smaller home."

The group was very happy to hear the news but they still feared the competition might not be able to continue. They agreed they'd all fight for the competition to continue. As the hungry crew devoured their mushroom stew, they saw Joshua coming up the hill.

"Where were you?" asked Caleb. "We were attacked by Endermen and Endermites."

"I didn't know there were any Endermen on the island," Joshua said quickly.

"Well, there are, or at least there were just now," replied Caleb. "Didn't you hear us call for help?"

"No, I was by the dock. I was repairing your boat that I destroyed," Joshua told Steve.

"Thanks," said Steve, "but if we don't stop this Endermen invasion, I might not be taking a boat home. I'll be destroyed by an Enderman and just respawn in my home and not be able to compete."

"That would be terrible," said Joshua coldly.

"Yes, it would," Sylvia said as she stared at Joshua.

Steve realized he wasn't the only person who didn't trust Joshua.

When they were done with the meal, the group parted ways. With a full energy bar, Steve was excited to work on his house. As he walked toward his patch of land, he decided to take a detour past the docks. Steve saw his boat with the gaping hole from the crash. It hadn't been repaired.

10
SOMETHING WICKED

As Steve worked on his home, he tried to convince himself that Joshua was innocent. Joshua had no reason to ruin the competition; he was Caleb's friend and was here to support him. Steve couldn't stop thinking about Thomas, the griefer, and how much trouble he'd caused his friends. There was something about Joshua that Steve didn't trust.

Steve constructed a large window that would look out on the sea. The house was turning out the way Steve envisioned, and he was so happy. With the Endermites gone, Steve was able to get a lot of work done. Yet he did take time off to build a pumpkin mask. He wanted to be prepared if there was another Endermen invasion.

A siren blasted throughout the island. Steve knew it was another announcement. Sylvia's voice boomed over a speaker: "Please meet at the stage for a feast. Everyone is invited."

Steve made his way toward the stage, and when he arrived he saw Sarah and Georgia chatting by the stage. Georgia was laughing.

"What's so funny?" asked Steve.

"I was telling Sarah about my crazy trip getting here. I was just about to tell her about how I had to figure out how to get here without a map," said Georgia.

"You know what?" said Sarah, "I lost my map too! I was so upset, but I still found my way here because—" but Sarah stopped talking when she saw Steve's face.

Steve stood frozen.

"What's the matter, Steve?" asked Georgia.

"I lost my map too," said Steve. "At first we blamed Max, but then it reappeared, so we forgot about it."

"Mine reappeared too!" exclaimed Sarah.

"So did mine!" said Georgia. "And there was no reason for it. I mean one minute it was missing and the next it was there. It was so crazy." Georgia couldn't believe Sarah and Steve had similar experiences.

"And we all forgot our coal," added Steve.

"It's amazing how much we have in common," remarked Sarah.

Steve was upset. "I don't think it's amazing. I think we are being tricked. Someone is sabotaging this contest."

Steve walked over to Caleb, who was talking to his friend Joshua, and asked them about their trip to the contest.

"Did you have any easy time getting here?" he asked.

"Super easy," Caleb remarked. "We had a map and it got us here no problem."

"Did you lose it at all?" asked Steve.

"No, we don't lose maps. We're very responsible," said Joshua.

"I'm responsible, and I lost my map," said Steve.

Joshua smiled. "Well, I'm glad you found your way here."

Steve excused himself and walked over to Max, Henry, Lucy, and Kyra.

"Hey, Steve!" said Lucy. "How's the house coming along?"

"I'm not worried about my house. I'm concerned about the competition. I suspect Joshua is trying to sabotage it."

"Why would he do that?" asked Henry.

"I don't know," said Steve, and then he told his friends about how the other contestants had experienced odd coincidences like the missing coal.

"It sounds like he's a griefer," remarked Max.

"We know how to deal with a griefer," added Henry.

"But I don't have time to watch him, because I have to build the house. Can you guys keep a close eye on him?" Steve asked his friends.

Steve didn't want to get distracted by a griefer. He just wanted to get back to work on his house. He had so many ideas for the inside. He was going to build a fireplace and a terrace off the second floor. Now that the foundation was done, he could really work on the details.

Steve's friends promised to keep a close eye on Joshua. Steve felt like everything was going to be okay, until he heard a shrill cry.

Sarah glanced at the sky and screamed. "Look!"

The Ender Dragon was flying toward them. Since they weren't in the End, somebody must have summoned this most evil powerful flying vulture. It could only be the work of a griefer. "There's another one behind it!" shouted Georgia.

The crowd sprinted toward the dorms for shelter. The Ender Dragons flew through the sky.

Steve followed his friends to the dorms as the Dragons flew overhead. Before a beast could strike him, he made it through the doors to safety. He sighed with relief as he formed a plan.

11
THE ENDER DRAGON
ISN'T THE END

Thump! A Dragon's wing banged into the side of the dorm, and the wall began to crumble. The group shielded themselves from the rubble.

Steve used his bow to shoot an arrow at the Dragon's stomach, which was visible from the hole in the wall.

"Bull's-eye!" Steve called out, but he knew one hit wouldn't affect the powerful beast.

"Everyone get your bows and arrows ready," instructed Henry.

"If we all hit it at the same time, we can defeat it!" said Steve.

The group was armed when the Dragon flew into the roof of the building. They shot a sea of arrows at the Dragon as dust and large parts of the roof fell near their feet.

"Don't take off your helmets," warned Lucy. "They will shield us from the crumbling building."

Steve knew Ender Dragons destroyed everything in their path. He hoped there were only two Dragons and they were just flying over the dorms. If one of the Dragons flew toward the houses the contestants were building, they'd be destroyed.

Their arrows hit the Dragon; it was getting weaker as the group continued attacking the flying monster.

Steve stood next to Joshua. He watched Joshua with his bow and arrows, fighting the Ender Dragon with the rest of the group. Joshua looked worried. Maybe Joshua wasn't the griefer. Steve was confused.

"This is a hard battle," Steve said to Joshua.

"Yes, but I like a challenge," replied Joshua.

Steve thought that was an odd comment.

More arrows hit the Dragon, and the group finally destroyed it. They shouted in glee as an egg was unleashed from the destroyed Dragon.

"There's still one more! We can't rejoice yet," said Henry.

"And there could be more on the way," added Joshua.

"I hope not!" cried Sarah.

The growls of another purple-eyed flying demon roared through the remains of the dorms.

"Here's the second one!" Lucy called out as she shot an arrow at the scaly black flesh.

The Dragon flew low to the ground and dug around the stage, instantly destroying it.

"I hope the houses we built are okay!" cried Georgia.

"If you're so talented, you should be able to rebuild it," Joshua said as he shot an arrow at the Dragon and it wailed.

"Building is hard and takes time," Steve told Joshua. Steve didn't trust Joshua at all.

The group tried to shoot as many arrows as fast as they could. Destroying the Ender Dragon was a challenge, since it was immune to water, lava, and potions. Their only advantage was that the Ender Dragon was spawned in the Overworld, which wasn't its normal environment. If they were fighting the Dragon in the End, the beast would be able to eat Ender Crystals and increase its energy levels.

"I think the arrows are weakening it!" Sarah said, since the beast seemed to lack the energy to flap its wings.

The Dragon's growls were growing quieter. Yet it still flew close to the dorms, destroying the last remaining wall. Now the group was exposed with only their armor to shield them. They held onto their bows and arrows, hoping they'd win this battle with the beast.

"Keep shooting at it!" Henry told them. "Don't give up."

The Ender Dragon let out a loud roar. It flapped its wings and flew close to the gang, almost landing on top of them.

Kyra was nervous. "It seems to be getting stronger!"

"No, that's not possible," Max told her.

Then the Dragon's wing hit a large mushroom. The Dragon let out one final roar and it was destroyed. Another egg dropped from the second destroyed Dragon.

Everyone took off their helmets and walked around to assess the damage this powerful Dragon had created on Mushroom Island.

The dorm was destroyed. The stage was destroyed. The island was covered in rubble.

"My friends and I can rebuild the stage and the dorms," Kyra told the judges.

"That's such a nice offer!" replied Sylvia.

"We'll help you," said Jonathan, and his fellow judges agreed. They would rebuild the structures needed for the contest while the builders went back to their sites to build their houses.

"Will you help us?" Kyra asked Joshua.

"Yes, of course. I'm a fantastic builder," replied Joshua.

"I'm sure you are," Steve told him. "You did a great job rebuilding my boat."

"Oh! I'm not done with your boat. Um . . . I'm still working on it," Joshua stuttered.

Joshua left with the others to start rebuilding the dorms and the contestants were able to return to their areas.

The contestants looked at each other with worried expressions. They all had the same thought circulating through their minds. They wondered if their homes were still standing. There wasn't that much time left before the judges would evaluate their work and there had been way too many distractions preventing them from building. They stood still. Nobody moved an inch.

Finally Steve took a deep breath and said, "I'm going to check out my house. I'm hoping the Dragon didn't get over to the building area."

Each step Steve took toward his building site seemed to take forever and filled him with dread. He walked past the mooshroom grazing and arrived at his house. It was fine! Steve was thrilled.

But then a siren rang throughout the island, followed by an announcement from Sylvia: "Please meet by the stage"—she paused—"That is, please meet where we used to have a stage."

Steve sprinted toward the stage area.

Sarah was crying. Georgia was crying. Caleb's lip quivered.

Joshua was talking to the judges.

Steve had a feeling in his gut that something was very wrong.

"How's your house?" Sarah asked Steve.

"Fine. But I'm guessing yours isn't."

Sylvia walked over to and questioned him: "Are you saying that your house has had no damage at all?"

Jonathan stood next to Sylvia and stated, "I find that very suspicious."

Steve knew he was being accused of something he didn't do. It reminded him of when the villagers believed he was the griefer who had been destroying his hometown, and he had needed to prove it was Thomas.

"Why?" Steve was innocent and shocked at this accusation. He wanted to tell them that he suspected Joshua to be the griefer, but the words wouldn't come out. He said, "I can't control the Ender Dragon."

Lexie's voice grew louder. "Steve, did you summon the Ender Dragon?"

"No, I'd never do anything like that," replied Steve. "Just ask my friends. They will tell you that I'm not a griefer."

"Your friends are treasure hunters," said Jonathan. "We know what treasure hunters do to get treasure. We can't trust them."

"But you have to trust me and my friends," pleaded Steve.

"We will let you participate in the contest, but we are watching you, Steve. If we find out that any of this is your fault, you will not only be asked to leave, but you'll be in serious trouble," Sylvia said sternly.

Steve couldn't believe his ears. Since the contest began, Steve had been worried about being attacked by a hostile mob and respawning in his home or having his house demolished by the Ender Dragon, but he never expected this to be the reason he'd leave the competition.

He knew what he had to do. He had to prove that he was innocent, and he had to build his dream house. Once he was able to clear his name and gain the respect of the judges, he'd be a winner, even if he didn't place first in the competition.

As he walked toward his house, he saw Georgia pass by. Steve called out to her but she didn't turn around. Steve was hurt. It seemed as if nobody believed him. He left to build his home—and rebuild his reputation.

12
BEGIN AGAIN

Steve knew how the others felt. They must have been heartbroken that all their hard work was destroyed. Steve recalled how upset he was when Thomas blew up his farm with TNT. The other contestants had to start all over again. Steve didn't think it was fair, since his house was almost done. He wanted to help the other contestants, but he knew that would be against the rules.

Steve began to place the final windows on his home and create large terraces with ocean views. Although the house was coming along quite nicely, Steve didn't feel like building. His heart wasn't in the contest anymore. After being accused of ruining the competition, he felt awful. Steve hated being wrongly accused. He wanted to clear his name. Luckily, he had friends who could help him.

While Steve adorned the walls of the home with emerald designs, he thought of ways Lucy, Max,

Henry, and Kyra could help him. Once he placed the last emerald on the house, he walked toward the dorm.

The gang was building the dorm with the judges.

"What are you doing here? Shouldn't you be building?" asked Sylvia.

"I just needed to talk to my friends for a minute," said Steve and Sylvia shook her head.

Lucy, Max, Henry, and Kyra approached Steve. Lucy blurted out, "Steve, everyone thinks you're the griefer. We tried to convince them you aren't, but they don't trust us either."

Kyra was upset. "I want to leave," she said. "I don't like being here when everyone is judging us."

"I need to prove I'm innocent, and I need your help."

"How can we help you?" asked Max. "We'll do anything."

"I want you to befriend Joshua and try to find out why he would do these things."

Before the gang could befriend Joshua, four Endermen appeared in the distance.

"Everyone get your pumpkin masks on right now!" Sylvia screamed.

The group grabbed the pumpkins from their inventories.

"Don't look in their direction." Jonathan's voice was shaky as he spoke, "Even with your masks on, look away."

Steve didn't listen. He shot forward toward the lanky creeping hostile mobs and struck one with his sword.

Max, Henry, Lucy, and Kyra followed. They struck the creatures.

The Endermen's loud sounds startled the group as they fought with all their might.

Henry hit the diamond sword into the flesh of an Enderman and a final knock destroyed it.

Georgia and Sarah must have heard the cries from the building area and jogged over with buckets of water, throwing them on the Endermen.

Splash! The Endermen were defeated.

"Thanks," Steve told them.

"I'm still not sure if you're the one who summoned all of this evil, but I want to finish this contest," said Sarah.

Looking at Steve, Georgia said, "Please, no more distractions."

"This isn't my fault!" Steve protested.

"We'll get to the bottom of this soon. Truthfully, I hope it isn't you, but if it is, I'll never forgive you," Georgia told him.

Steve followed Sarah and Georgia and went to finish his house. He hoped his friends could help him solve his problem. He was about to reach his building site when he heard panicked screams coming from the stage area. He sprinted back and found everyone with swords out. Although there were eight of them, the beast they were fighting had three heads.

Sarah, Georgia, and Caleb rushed toward the stage.

"What's going on, Steve?" asked Sarah.

They didn't wait for an answer. Everyone saw a flash of blue and the deafening sound of an explosion. The half-built dorm was torn to pieces.

The black three-headed Wither had spawned, shooting Wither Skulls at the group, who tried to protect themselves by seeking shelter underneath a nearby enormous mushroom. It was useless; the beast unleashed its barrage of skeletons, and there was no place to hide. They had to fight.

Steve raced toward the monster with his diamond sword. He wanted to save the day, but one person was no match for such a powerful menace.

Max, Lucy, Henry, and Kyra raced toward Steve to join him in battle. Dressed in armor, they shot arrows at the Wither, hoping it would weaken the creature. The Wither just crushed the partially built stage.

"How are you going to win this battle?" Kyra asked the group. The Wither cornered her and shot a Wither Skull in her direction. She was about to be hit. Kyra closed her eyes and braced herself for the punch.

When nothing happened, she opened her eyes. "What happened?" she asked.

"Look!" Steve's voice was breathless with exhaustion. "It has a new enemy."

An army of Endermen with gaping mouths making piercing sounds stood in front of the Wither. It was a battle of the mobs.

13
FIGHT IN THE SKY

The Endermen's eyes glowed as the sun began to set and darkness fell upon Mushroom Island.

The Wither shot Wither Skulls at the Endermen as they lurked toward the Wither. A group of Endermen teleported toward the Wither and struck him, but the Wither's energy was high and it fought back, unleashing more Wither Skulls that hit the Endermen.

"Maybe they can battle this on their own?" Kyra asked hopefully.

Max looked up at the sky. "No! Look!"

"Not again!" Henry cried as he saw an Ender Dragon's purple eyes in the dark sky.

"Someone needs to light a torch," Henry told the group.

Caleb got a torch. "But I need my hands to hold my bow and arrow," he cried out.

Max walked over to the one remaining wall of the rebuilt dorm. "Place the torch on this wall," he suggested.

In the light, the gang watched the Ender Dragon swoop down, avoiding the Wither Skulls the powerful Wither shot at the flying creature.

The Ender Dragon flew into the sky as the Wither rose up from the ground, advancing toward the Dragon. The masterful three-headed beast skyrocketed toward its winged enemy, still shooting Wither Skulls at the Dragon.

The Dragon was hit but not defeated. Growling and roaring, it soared higher. With an open mouth, the Dragon lunged toward the Wither. The attack made the Wither turn red. The battle intensified in the sky, but the group didn't have time to watch this competition between the two bosses because they had their own battle. They had to battle the now unoccupied Endermen.

The Endermen teleported toward the group as sounds of the Dragon and the Wither's battle echoed.

Steve and Henry ran toward the mobs with swords as the rest of the gang placed pumpkins on their heads and went in search of water.

The group sprinted toward the water, but before they reached the shoreline, there was a loud boom!

"What's that?" Kyra asked nervously.

Boom! The sound was louder and followed by a bolt of lightning.

"It's going to rain!" Lucy said joyfully.

Steve was in the middle of an intense battle with the Endermen when the first drops of rain poured down on him and destroyed the long-legged pests.

"Raindrops never felt so good," Steve said to Henry as he brushed the rain from his face.

The storm grew stronger and so did the battle between the Wither and the Ender Dragon. Neither were affected by water and they continued to chase each other. Both of these creatures were very strong and the battle wasn't going to be quick.

The Dragon flew fast and dodged many of the Wither Skulls, but it was no match for the Wither. Its three heads shot Wither Skulls from its mouth almost instantly, and it was on the Dragon's tail. The Dragon roared and struck the Wither with its wing and for a moment the Wither turned red. The Wither flew up through the rain, narrowly avoiding a lightning bolt that shot through the stormy sky.

"I wish we had shelter," Lucy said as she looked at the hostile battle in the sky and tried to cover herself from the rain.

Kyra began to build a house out of the mushrooms. "Mushroom houses don't take that long to build. Let's make them together."

The group gathered red mushrooms and bone meal. They began to construct the floors as they attached ladders and used a torch to light up the interior of the home. They worked as fast as they could in the rain. Once the rain stopped more Endermen could spawn, and they needed a shelter from them.

Everyone's house was completed but Joshua's. He didn't have any bones in his inventory to make bone meal. Steve could see him searching for something to help him craft the home.

"Do you need any bones?" Steve asked Joshua.

"I'm fine. I don't need any help from you," Joshua replied as he walked toward Caleb's house.

Steve could hear Joshua asking Caleb if he had any space for two beds. Then Joshua walked into Caleb's mushroom house.

"Everyone finished?" Kyra looked at the group.

"Yes," the group called out in unison as they made their way into the comfort of their mushroom shelters, safe from monsters but still able to see the show in the stormy sky.

The raindrops fell against Steve's roof as he watched the Ender Dragon bang into the Wither.

The Wither unleashed more Wither Skulls and the Dragon seemed to be growing weaker as it flew closer to the ground. At times it looked as if it was about to fall to the ground but it didn't. The Dragon seemed to grow stronger as it flew toward the Wither, and with a final blow, it destroyed the three-headed monster as a Nether Star fell from the sky.

Although Steve watched the battle and cheered when he saw the Wither was defeated and the Ender Dragon had won, he also knew this meant they were the Ender Dragon's next victims.

"Fire your arrows!" Steve encouraged the group.

The group got out their weapons and aimed at the Dragon. The arrows struck its underbelly, and the Dragon dropped an egg and was destroyed.

The powerful Dragon might have been the winner of the battle of the boss, but it was a short-lived victory.

Finally the rain stopped. Steve and the gang made their way toward the rubble where the stage was being rebuilt.

"I think it's safe now," Steve told them.

A roar boomed in the distance.

"Not again!" Georgia cried out.

14

THE BATTLE OF THE BUILDERS

"How many Ender Dragons do you see?" Georgia asked as she peeked out from her mushroom house.

Sarah looked at the sky. "I see three!"

"Who is doing this?" Georgia was mad. She wanted the competition to continue.

Sylvia, Lexie, and Jonathan stood with their bows and arrows out, ready for battle.

"We can't worry about who started it," Caleb told them. "We just have to fight until it's over."

Steve didn't agree. "If we find out who did this, we can get them to stop and we can end this pointless battle."

But Steve's words were lost when the three Ender Dragons flew through the air. Their wings flapped as they gathered up speed and headed toward the group standing beside their mushroom houses.

The mooshrooms grazing behind them looked up at the hostile mob.

The three Dragons charged at the players and swooped down. One struck Sylvia.

"Are you okay?" Steve asked as he shot an arrow at the Dragon.

"Yes," she said softly. Sylvia was hurt but still alive.

The second Dragon hit Caleb's mushroom house, destroying the roof. *Boom!* The third Dragon hit the side of the mushroom house. Caleb and Joshua tried to fight them off with arrows.

"Stop!" Joshua screamed. "Don't attack me!"

The Dragons didn't listen. They growled at Joshua and he sped away from the house, leaving Caleb to battle the Dragons on his own.

"Joshua!" Caleb screamed, but Joshua didn't turn back. Caleb shot an arrow at the Dragon, but he was no match for the three hostile beasts that were now cornering him.

Caleb shot a second arrow just as the Dragons lunged toward him.

"Help!" he cried out.

Steve and the group ran toward Caleb and started shooting their arrows, hoping to weaken the Dragons. One of the Dragon's three-toed black feet hit the side of Caleb's mushroom house as the Dragon steadied itself for flight and tried to avoid the barrage of arrows.

Caleb was lucky. The Ender Dragons had a better enemy to battle. Another Wither!

The three Dragons flew through the skies away from the group toward a Wither. They surrounded the Wither, attacking it from each angle until it was destroyed and another Nether Star dropped down by the gang.

"Uh-oh, now we're next!" cried Lucy.

"But we will battle this together," Steve reassured them.

Max looked down and saw more Endermites. "Oh no!" he said, and leapt toward two with his diamond sword.

"And more Endermen!" announced Sarah as the group put on their pumpkin masks.

"Lead them to the water!" Henry instructed Steve and Caleb.

Steve and Caleb took off their masks and the Endermen's mouths gaped open and shrieked.

"They're teleporting!" Steve shouted to Caleb and they leapt toward the water, where the Endermen fell in.

As Steve and Caleb swam to the shore, they could see Joshua aboard Max's pirate ship.

"Joshua!" Caleb called out, but Joshua didn't turn around. He navigated the boat toward the sea.

"Let's follow him!" Steve said, and the duo hurried toward the pier, hopped onto Henry's sailboat, and raced after Joshua.

Steve navigated the boat in Joshua's direction; they picked up speed and came to the side of the pirate ship.

"Where are you going?" Caleb shouted.

"I'm leaving," said Joshua. He didn't look at his friend but instead he attempted to increase the speed of his boat.

Steve sped up. The two boats raced as Steve jumped aboard the boat Joshua had stolen from Max. Joshua was shocked when Steve took out his diamond sword.

"This is my friend Max's boat," said Steve. He held the diamond sword, pointing it at Joshua.

"I'm sorry," said Joshua. He could barely get the words out. His lips quivered.

"What is your problem?! You hit my boat. You stole Max's boat. And you abandoned your friend."

"I don't know," replied Joshua.

Steve inched forward, bringing his sword closer to Joshua. "I don't believe you; I've met people like you before."

Joshua moved back from Steve. "What does that mean?" he asked. The boat was barely moving.

Caleb abandoned the other boat and hopped aboard the ship with Joshua and Steve. "You aren't my friend anymore, Joshua!"

Joshua was cornered. There was no escape. They were at sea and he was outnumbered.

"Stop! Stop!" Joshua screamed. "You're right, it's all my fault."

Caleb was shocked. "Why?"

"I was jealous. I wanted to be a part of the contest," Joshua confessed.

The Ender Dragon's roar could be heard in the distance. Steve was worried about his friends.

"Because of your jealousy, my best friends are fighting the battle of their lives, and you ruined a competition that I had been looking forward to for a long time!" Steve screamed at Joshua.

"I wasn't chosen for the contest!" Joshua screamed back.

"Do you only care about yourself?" asked Caleb.

"No!" yelled Joshua.

Henry's sailboat was drifting farther out to sea. Soon it would be lost.

Caleb looked out at the boat. "Look what you did to Henry's boat! If we didn't have to chase after you, it would be at the dock."

"The boat!" said Steve in frustration. "That's just one of the many things. You summoned the Wither and the Ender Dragon."

"And the Endermites and Endermen!" added Caleb.

"Can't you see how much damage and chaos you've caused? Just because you didn't get into a competition!" Steve shook his head.

"You have to put an end to this," Caleb warned Joshua.

"I don't know how," Joshua could barely spit out the words.

"I should never have brought you here," moaned Caleb.

Boom! A blast was heard in the distance.

"I feel so helpless. I need to be there for my friends." Steve was very upset. "There has to be something you can do, Joshua. We're taking you back to Mushroom Island."

"I want you to tell everybody what you've done. And you will make it better," Caleb told him as Steve guided the boat back to the shores of Mushroom Island.

"I don't know how I can fix it, I really don't," Joshua said and then tried to jump overboard just as Steve docked the boat.

"No!" Caleb shouted as he grabbed Joshua.

The Ender Dragon flew down toward Joshua and struck him. "See, I can't stop him!" said Joshua.

"Get out your bow and arrow," Steve told him. Joshua obeyed and the three shot arrows as they tried to make their escape from the winged beast.

15

REUNITED

Steve, Caleb, and Joshua battled the Ender Dragon. When it was defeated, Steve called out, "I need to find my friends!" and ran toward the center of Mushroom Island. Caleb and Joshua followed him.

Steve found his friends in the middle of a battle with another Ender Dragon. The three joined the others and helped them battle the boss. The Dragon was weak and within seconds it exploded, leaving a purple aura and dropping an egg.

"It's going to be okay!" Steve announced.

"There could be another Ender Dragon approaching," Lucy said. Her voice was weak and she sounded exhausted.

"Joshua," Steve said while looking over at the griefer, "please inform them of what you did."

Joshua put his head down. "I did nothing. I have no idea what you're talking about Steve."

Sylvia came forward, "Please Steve, don't blame this on Joshua. We know you have summoned these beasts to destroy the contest."

Steve was shocked. "Why would I do that? I wanted to be a part of the competition."

"Well, your house wasn't destroyed," said Jonathon.

Henry defended his friend. "My friend, Steve, would never do anything like that!"

"Henry, ask him where your boat is. He destroyed it," Joshua blurted out.

"That's a lie. It got lost at sea while we were chasing you," said Steve.

Henry was upset. "My boat is gone?"

Kyra stood next to Steve. "I worked so hard building all those boats. But after the way you treated Steve's boat, I don't trust you, Joshua."

"You should trust me," Joshua told them, "I'm innocent. Steve is the one who is causing all of this trouble."

"Steve, we're going to have to ask you to leave the competition, and you will be banned from Mushroom Island forever," announced Lexie.

Steve looked at Lucy, Max, Henry, and Kyra. "Okay, guys, I guess we have to leave."

"But we know you're innocent, Steve," said Kyra.

"Prove it," Joshua said smugly.

"I can't." Steve put his head down and was ready to surrender. He just wanted to go home, back to the wheat farm to see Snuggles, Rufus, and Jasmine.

He didn't want to be in a competition where people blamed him for things he'd never do.

"Steve isn't the griefer!" exclaimed Henry.

"We're not leaving until you are proven innocent," Lucy told him.

"You can't give up," said Max, "we're not. We're going to prove that you aren't behind this and expose whoever caused all of this trouble."

Steve was shocked when Sarah and Georgia stood with Henry, Lucy, Max, and Kyra. "We also believe you're innocent and will prove it," Sarah announced.

"Really?" asked Steve. He was so happy to see that his new friends Sarah and Georgia stood by him.

Caleb walked into the center of the group. "I can't watch this anymore. I have to say something."

"Stop!" Joshua called out to him.

"I'm sorry, Joshua. I can't defend you. I have to be honest with everyone."

"Caleb, you're making a big mistake," warned Joshua.

"Being honest is never a mistake," Caleb told him.

"But—" Joshua tried to speak, but Caleb interrupted him.

"I'm sorry, Joshua. I have to be honest. Steve was right, it was Joshua who summoned all the hostile mobs. He's a griefer. I didn't believe it at first, but when I realized he was the one causing all of this trouble, he tried to escape by stealing Max's boat," confessed Caleb.

"My boat!" cried Max.

"Don't worry, your boat is fine; it's at the dock. But this competition has been ruined," said Caleb.

Joshua stood by the half-demolished mushroom house. "I'm sorry. I really am. I just wanted to be chosen for the contest. When Caleb was asked to participate and I wasn't chosen, I was really upset."

"Upset!" Sylvia called out, "that's putting it mildly."

Jonathan looked at Joshua. "You ruined the contest!"

"And you guys wrongly accused my friend," Kyra told the judges.

"We apologize, Steve," Sylvia said, "but you can see how we thought it was you."

"But there wasn't any real proof and you asked me to leave the contest!" Steve was in tears.

A lone Ender Dragon flew toward the crowd.

"Stop it!" cried Lucy.

"I can't, I have no control over it anymore," Joshua confessed.

"If you let me know how you summoned it, I think I can help you stop it with command blocks," said Henry. "Where are you spawning it from?"

"I have someone stepping on a pressure plate activating a command block on one of the jungle trees at the shore of the jungle biome. That's why I was going on the boat—I was trying to get them to stop," said Joshua.

"We need to get on a boat now," demanded Henry. "Come with us, Steve."

As the Ender Dragon swooped between them and leapt at Caleb, Joshua pushed him out of the way.

Lucy shot an arrow. It hit the Dragon's side and the beast exploded; another egg dropped from the sky.

Lucy remarked, "I used to think destroying the Ender Dragon was the biggest challenge, but now it seems so easy."

"I wouldn't use the word easy," said Kyra.

"Joshua, you need to stop this at once," demanded Lucy. "Go on the ship now!"

Steve, Henry, Joshua, and Caleb sprinted toward the shore. As they boarded Max's boat, they saw another boat approaching and a familiar face in the distance.

"Eli!" Steve called out.

16
COMMAND BLOCKS

Steve stood at the edge of the boat looking out at the large trees growing on the shoreline. "I see the jungle biome!" he shouted.

"Do you know where your griefer friend is? We don't have time to lose." Caleb was breathless. He was losing energy.

"Yes, he's in a tree right off the shore," replied Joshua.

"I hope you're telling the truth," said Henry.

They docked the boat on the shore and walked into the thick of the jungle. A wild ocelot raced by them, but Steve ignored it as he followed Joshua to the other griefer. Joshua led them through the leafy landscape. It was hard to see, and Steve was worried that Joshua would try to escape. Henry trailed behind Joshua, keeping a close eye on him.

"Where are we going?" asked Steve. It seemed like Joshua was taking them in circles.

"I don't trust this guy," said Henry.

"It's just a few more feet," promised Joshua.

"I hope so. It's so hard to see anything," said Steve.

Caleb took out shears from his inventory and cut a path for them.

"This was a great idea, Caleb!" exclaimed Joshua. "Now I can see the tree."

Steve looked up and saw someone the color of a rainbow seated in a tree. He had seen that griefer before when he was alone in the Nether. Now, the griefer stuck out in the green leaves.

"I know that man!" announced Steve.

"You do?" Joshua was shocked.

"Yes, he tried to attack me in the Nether."

"Stop him, Joshua!" said Caleb.

"Stop!" Joshua called to the griefer.

"Joshua?" The rainbow person called down from the tree.

"We have to end this game. It's hurting too many people," said Joshua.

"No!" the rainbow man said defiantly.

"Come down now! I order you!" screamed Joshua.

The rainbow man laughed. "Never! I am going to destroy Mushroom Island."

"Not on my watch," Henry shouted, and he shot an arrow just as the rainbow man jumped to another part of the tree to avoid it.

"You have no idea how much fun I'm having," the rainbow man taunted them.

"You've unleashed so many Ender Dragons. What are you planning on doing next? Haven't you had your fill of fun?" asked Steve. He slowly began to climb the tree.

The rainbow man shot an arrow at Steve, but he jumped down to dodge it. "Don't come up here," the rainbow man warned.

"You've gone too far!" Henry shouted, shooting an arrow.

Joshua screamed at the rainbow man, "I command you to stop!" Joshua took out his bow and arrow and shot at the rainbow man, who jumped down from the tree to avoid being hit. The rainbow man stood in front of Steve, Henry, Caleb, and Joshua.

"I've met you before, and I know how bad you are," Steve told him while clutching his diamond sword.

"Game over!" said Joshua, as he pointed his bow and arrow at the rainbow man.

"Not until I say so." The rainbow man took out his diamond sword and leapt at Joshua.

Steve ran toward the rainbow man and struck the griefer with his diamond sword, destroying him with one hit.

"Now the game is over," announced Steve.

"Good job!" Henry told Steve.

Caleb and Joshua stood on the path by the tree. Steve looked out at the boat on the shore and was relieved to see it was still there. He just wanted to get back to Mushroom Island and finish the contest.

"Now that he's gone, what are you going to do to me?" Joshua asked nervously.

"You get a chance to start again. I can't hurt anyone who isn't a threat to me anymore," Steve told him.

"Steve, let's go back to Mushroom Island," said Caleb.

"What about me?" asked Joshua.

"You're not invited," Caleb told him. "I think it's for the best if we just part ways."

"But you're one of my best friends," said Joshua.

"You aren't a friend," Caleb said as he, Steve, and Henry walked toward the boat and made their way back to Mushroom Island.

"You don't know what true friends are. I feel bad for you," Henry remarked to Joshua as he walked away.

"Now we can finally finish the competition," said Steve as Mushroom Island came into sight.

"Finish!" Caleb laughed, "I think you mean start. Everything was destroyed."

"Yes, I have to see if my house is still standing after the last Ender Dragon attack."

The shore was in sight, and they could see the gang by the docks. As they docked the boat, they were greeted by all of their friends.

"We have some mushroom stew for you guys," said Lucy. "We figured you must have used up a lot of energy."

"And Steve and Caleb need their energy for the competition. There's only one day left," Sylvia said as she served them stew.

"One day!" exclaimed Steve.

He ate the stew as fast as his mouth could take in the tasty meal. He had a house to finish—if it was still standing!

17

COMPETITION AND AWARDS

Steve walked toward his house. With each step, his anxiety worsened. What if his house was destroyed? How would he build a proper house in one day? Yes, he could build a mushroom house, but not a house worthy of winning a medal.

He took a deep breath before he arrived at the site. Steve looked at the rubble where his house once stood.

"And to think, they were going to kick me out of the contest because my house wasn't destroyed," Steve said to himself and laughed.

Yet there was no time to waste. He quickly used all the resources he had in his inventory. This time he wasn't worried that somebody would steal his coal, and he could build without worrying about hostile mobs, too.

Steve built the walls and was satisfied with the structure. Steve was really skilled at decorating the house with intricate emerald designs on the walls of the living room.

Sylvia stood outside the door of the house and called out to Steve. "Looks like you're doing a good job. We're just going around to check on everyone's progress. I assume your house was destroyed after all."

"Yes," Steve said as he put windows in the home.

"I want to apologize for the way we behaved. We had no right to ask you to leave the competition."

"I was really upset about it," said Steve without looking up. He had a terrace to build.

"Well, I'll let you get back to work. I was just making sure everything was okay and I wanted to apologize."

Steve finished the house. It wasn't the grand house he'd envisioned when he was asked to participate, but it was the best he could do given the time frame. He was excited to see the other homes too. Although he really wanted to come in first place and still dreamed of walking away with a gold medal around his neck, he'd made some new friends, so Steve was happy for the experience.

The siren went off, followed by Sylvia's announcement: "Contestants, please stop building. Your time is up. Please meet us at the stage. And let the judging begin!"

Steve sprinted toward the stage. He couldn't believe what a fantastic job Lucy, Max, Henry, and Kyra had done rebuilding the stage.

Henry patted his friend on the back. "Good luck, Steve!"

"Thanks!"

Sylvia stood on the stage with Lexie and Jonathan.

"Today we are judging a contest we thought was never going to be completed. These contestants have been through a lot. We all have. But now we'll see what they built despite all of the problems that plagued this contest."

The judges led everyone to Sarah's house. It was inspired by Mushroom Island. It was a large red mushroom, and the home went very deep underground.

"I call this house Mushroom Mining Mansion," explained Sarah. "It goes so deep underground, it doubles as a mine. I was inspired to build this house after mining for coal and having to build a mushroom house during a rainstorm while being attacked by an Ender Dragon."

The group applauded.

They toured Georgia's house next. It was a log home and stood on the shoreline with a large picture window to look out at the water. They went inside to see the colorful carpets and the fireplaces.

"I named this house Lookout Lodge because I placed a large window where you can enjoy the view and also look out for your friends."

The next home was Caleb's. It was shaped like a ship. You had to use a ladder to climb inside.

"I call this Seaside Estate," said Caleb as he showed the group his work. "I haven't tested it out yet, so I'm not sure it's seaworthy. I like the idea of a home that has multiple uses."

The group then made their way to Eli's house. It was a wooden house with a large deck. Although the interior was empty, there were a few beds.

"First of all, I can't believe I even made it back here in time," Eli said. "I call this house Decked Out. When I was on my way back, I realized that I wanted to build a house with a big deck so you can see everything that's going on and be around people. I love the idea of being home, yet being outdoors."

Steve's was the final house to be judged. Everyone crowded around Steve's cobblestone home with the large windows and terrace. He invited them inside to see the emerald designs on the living room wall. Outside, the mooshroom grazed peacefully.

"I just call this place Home Away from Home. As some of you know, it looks very similar to my house on my wheat farm, where I live with cows, sheep, and pigs. I love the idea of having animals close by and I also like using emeralds to decorate my home."

The judges led everyone back to the stage, where Sylvia made an announcement. "The judges need to meet alone. Please come back tonight for a feast and the announcement of the winner."

Steve walked back to his home. He stood on the terrace and looked out at the shore. This had been quite an adventure. He wondered if he'd be the winner.

"Steve," Kyra called to him.

"Can we come in?" asked Henry.

"Sure," Steve replied and Kyra, Lucy, Max, and Henry walked into the house.

"Are you excited for the feast?" asked Lucy.

"I bet he's nervous," Henry said.

"I hope you win!" said Kyra.

"Me too," Steve said.

The siren went off. Sylvia announced the feast was starting. Everyone left Steve's house and made their way to the feast.

It was the last night on Mushroom Island, and the feast was the farewell party.

Sylvia stood on the stage. "This was a hard contest to judge," she started.

Jonathan added, "Every house was excellent and well planned, but we could only choose one first place winner."

Lexie held the medal, "We would like to present this medal to—"

Boom!

The group looked around, prepared for anything.

"Not again!" Jonathan called out.

Boom! It was thunder. Raindrops fell as Lexie said, "The winner is Sarah, for Mushroom Mining Mansion."

Everyone cheered. The thunder boomed! The rain didn't stop the party.

"Congratulations!" Steve told Sarah, as they feasted in the rain.

18
SAIL AWAY

The next morning was sunny. The rain had ended, and so had the contest. Steve and the gang spent the night in the house he built.

"I know you didn't win, but I really like this house. I wish we could stay here longer," said Kyra.

"We have to leave today," said Steve. "I think they're having another contest."

"Despite everything that happened, I had a lot of fun," said Kyra.

"You'd make a great treasure hunter, Kyra. You have serious survival skills," remarked Henry.

"Really?" Kyra didn't believe him.

"Yes, you should come treasure hunting with us!" Lucy said with excitement.

"Aren't you guys coming back to the wheat farm with me?" asked Steve.

"When we found the jungle temple, I realized I missed treasure hunting. I need to go on a treasure hunt," said Henry.

"Come with us, Steve," said Max.

"I think I've had enough adventure after this contest. I want to check on my farm."

"But it will be fun," Lucy said.

"I'll go back to the farm and watch Jasmine, Snuggles, and Rufus. When you're done with your adventure, you can tell me all about it. I can't wait to hear about all the awesome treasures you'll discover," said Steve. He knew he wanted to go home.

"If I go with them, will you check on my house?" asked Kyra.

"Of course," replied Steve, "I'll check on it every day until you come home."

"Before we go, I have to build more boats." With that, Kyra headed to the dock. She had a lot of work ahead of her since Joshua had destroyed Steve's boat and Henry's boat was lost at sea.

The group joined Kyra at the dock and helped her build.

Sylvia, Jonathan, and Lexie walked over to Kyra and watched her work.

"You're quite the builder, Kyra. Maybe you'll be invited to participate in the contest next time," said Sylvia.

When the boats were finished, Sarah, Georgia, Caleb, and Eli all stood on the dock.

"I'll come visit you at the wheat farm," said Georgia.

"I want everyone to visit me," Steve announced. He was so glad to have made new friends, but also sad to leave them.

Steve said goodbye to Kyra, who left with Max, Lucy, and Henry.

At last, Steve hopped aboard his boat. Although he was disappointed he didn't leave Mushroom Island as a winner, he knew there would be other contests and he was happy to be sailing back home.

The End

ALSO AVAILABLE FROM SKY PONY PRESS

The Quest for the Diamond Sword

A Minecraft Gamer's Adventure

By Winter Morgan

Steve lives on a wheat farm and likes to spend his mornings in the village and trade his wheat for emeralds, armor, books, swords, and food. One morning, he finds that zombies have attacked the villagers. The zombies have also turned the village blacksmith into a zombie, leaving Steve without a place to get swords. To protect himself and the few villagers that remain, Steve goes on a quest to mine for forty diamonds, which are the most powerful mineral in the Overworld. He wants to craft these diamonds into a diamond sword to shield him and the villagers from the zombies.

Far from his home, with night about to set in, Steve fears for his life. Nighttime is when users are most vulnerable in Minecraft. As he looks for shelter in a temple, he meets a trio of treasure hunters, Max, Lucy, and Henry, who are trying to unearth the treasure under the temple. Steve tells them of his master plan to mine for the most powerful mineral in the Overworld—the diamond. The treasure hunters are eager to join him. Facing treacherous mining conditions, a thunderstorm, and attacks from hostile mobs, these four friends question if it's better to be a single player than a multiplayer as they try to watch out for each other and chase Steve's dream at the same time.

Will Steve find the diamonds? Will his friends help or hinder the search? Should he trust his new treasure hunter friends? And will Steve get back in time to save the villagers?

$7.99 paperback • ISBN 978-1-63220-442-4

ALSO AVAILABLE FROM SKY PONY PRESS

The Mystery of the Griefer's Mark

A Minecraft Gamer's Adventure, Book Two

By Winter Morgan

Steve is back and ready for more adventures! But this time the excitement lands closer to home. While walking home from the village, Steve is surprised to hear a loud *BOOM!* When he arrives, he finds his wheat farm destroyed and a huge crater where the wheat once grew. And his diamond sword is missing! Steve believes it's the act of a griefer with a lot of TNT. Devastated, Steve wants to rebuild and find his sword, but with his wheat destroyed, he must call on old friends to help him.

All together again, Lucy, Max, and Henry tell harrowing stories of their treasure hunts and conquests, and Steve discusses his strategy for rebuilding. They all go to sleep, excited to begin their plans. But when they wake up, Henry is missing!

Who is the griefer terrorizing Steve and the villagers? And how will Steve find the resources to rebuild his prosperous farm? With suspicion circulating and no answers to be found, Steve finds himself wrongly suspected of these crimes—and so he must find his friend and discover who the mischievous griefer is before something even worse happens.

$7.99 paperback • ISBN 978-1-63220-726-5

Invasion of the Overworld

Book One in the Gameknight999 Series: An Unofficial Minecrafter's Adventure

By Mark Cheverton

Gameknight999 loved Minecraft, but above all else he loved to grief—to intentionally ruin the gaming experience for other users.

When one of his father's inventions teleports him into the game, Gameknight is forced to live out a real-life adventure inside a digital world. What will happen if he's killed? Will he respawn? Die in real life? Stuck in the game, Gameknight discovers Minecraft's best-kept secret, something not even the game's programmers realize: the creatures within the game are alive! He will have to stay one step ahead of the sharp claws of zombies and pointed fangs of spiders, but he'll also have to learn to make friends and work as part of a team if to have any chance of surviving the Minecraft war his arrival has started.

This action-packed tribute to the worldwide computer game phenomenon is a runaway publishing smash and the perfect companion for Minecraft fans of all ages.

$9.99 paperback • ISBN 978-1-63220-711-1